WASHOE COUNTY LIBRARY

3 1235 01003 4564

10/
95

J
Fiction
HAR

SIERRA VIEW BRANCH LIBRARY

CHILDREN'S
COLLECTION
827-0169

D0690023

Property Of
County Library

J
Fiction
HAR

DATE

FEB 08 1998

3 1235 01003 4564

WASHOE COUNTY LIBRARY

THE STORM

Marc Harshman

Illustrated by Mark Mohr

COBBLEHILL BOOKS
Dutton/New York

 SCHOOL had gone just fine until then. Just an everyday class. And just like the beginning of every tornado season, the teacher began going over the usual information about the safety drill and then the storms themselves. After she explained the map of school exits, she showed a few slides of real tornadoes. Next she described what to do if caught outside in one. It was then Roger had piped up.

"It must be real scary for Jonathan!"

"Jonathan stuck in his wheelchair is what he means," Jonathan muttered to himself.

This was what he hated. Just this. Being singled out. Different. And of all things, a storm. There were things he was scared of, but storms weren't one of them. He loved storms. He loved those evenings when he and Dad would watch a thunderstorm, and its spidering lightning, boom and flash the darkness into daylight.

What he was scared of was much more common and everyday. Cars. Traffic. The squealing of tires on pavement. He could still see, as if in a freeze-frame, the red truck the second before it blindsided him as he crossed US 40 under the flashing red light. And he was scared of moments like these, around others, when he realized everyone was thinking about him, or not really him, but his "condition"—his legs, his inability to use them, his wheelchair. He hated these moments when he felt everyone looking at him. He dreaded this as much as the flashbacks because this happened more often.

The rest of the class went on about funnel clouds and the conditions that caused them, how their ground speeds could reach sixty, and the winds inside them over two hundred miles per hour. Jonathan knew all this and he daydreamed while the class went over what he had heard before. He even yawned.

Jonathan didn't know it but people were yawning everywhere that day. And George Richardson's bunions were hurting him "something awful." Meg Thomas complained there wasn't a "breath of wind" to dry her washing. Cattle had lain down at midday at Whitesel's. "Storm's comin." "Gonna rain." "Bad weather."

"What I really hate is this heat!" Jonathan complained to no one in particular as he wheeled himself away from the bus and down the long drive to the house. "Everything sticks to me in this chair." He was happy, though, to see his mom on the porch, knowing that she now understood about not meeting him at the bus.

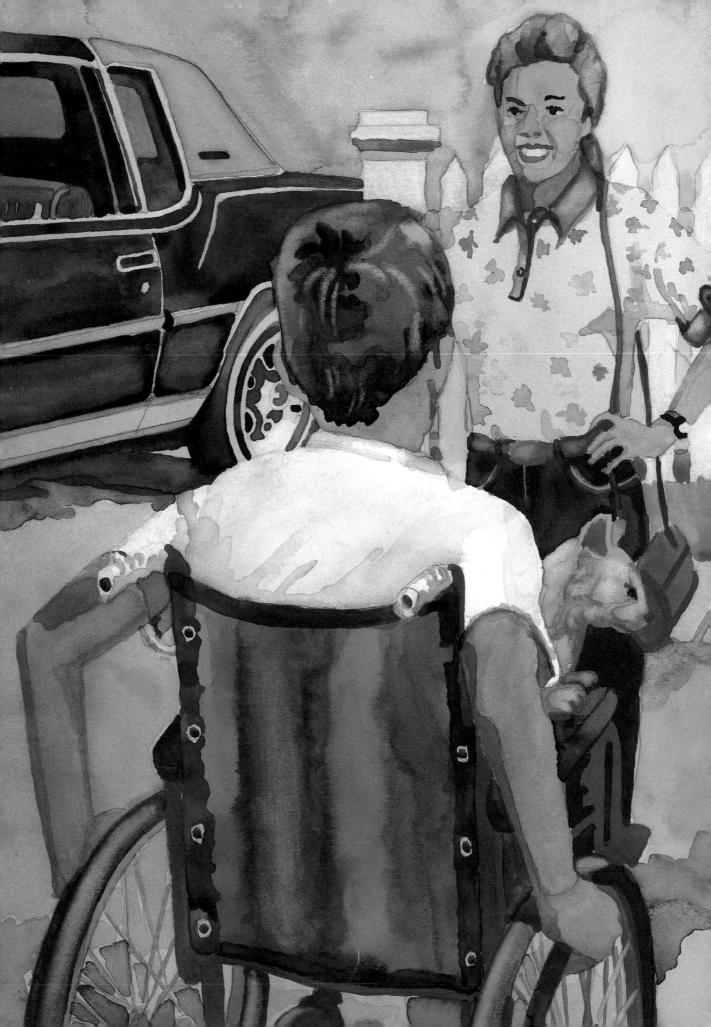

 "Jonathan, this car's giving me fits again. Dale said he'd take a look at it if I brought it in right away. I should be back in plenty of time, but supper is made if I'm not. Just put it in the oven. Your dad's still at Reynold's working on that roof. I've got the cows in the barn and the chickens fed. Storm's comin', Martha told me, and she's never wrong. Oh, and if I run late, could you get the horses?"

"Sure, Mom," he smiled. "Don't worry, I'll take care of them."

Ducking into the car, she yelled, "Thanks!" and drove off.

Ever since the accident, Jonathan had done everything he could, and his therapists as well, to make the rest of his body as strong as possible. Mom and Dad had helped a lot, too—making changes in the house, adding ramps outside, putting rope handles on the barn doors low enough to reach. They had even adjusted the horse halters so it was easier for him to snap on a lead rope. It all helped.

Since he was already out, he decided to go ahead and whistle the horses into the lot. It wasn't easy but a short while later he was rolling himself back out of the root cellar toward the horse trough, carrots lain carefully across his lap.

As usual, Buster was first. Buster was his, the one he had hand-fed since a colt. Buster nickered and then nuzzled at his hand so hard he nearly spilled the carrots. "You want sugar, I know, but it's staying in my pockets for now."

Back in the barn he turned on Dad's milking radio:

"A line of thunderstorms approaching east-central Indiana could have severe hail and lightning and a tornado watch has been issued for Wayne, Randolph, Jay, and Delaware counties."

He'd heard this before. A "watch" meant there was a chance, nothing more—it seemed there were dozens every spring. Only the warnings got his attention. This did mean, though, that there was a good chance of a storm and Jonathan liked any kind of storm.

He put his hands to the rubber rims and pushed himself out the west doors. There were ripples in the grass and the skies had clouded. It was peaceful. Since his accident he felt more alert somehow. He liked watching those ripples in the grass, the tumbling of the clouds overhead, the way the fluffy tops of the sycamores by the creek bent and tossed in the rising wind.

But. That rising wind. He wasn't sure he liked the low wail that began moving through the farmyard, nor the green-yellow tint of the sky. They were signs the old-timers said meant "twister."

"Better get busy and see to closing things up," he told himself. "Who knows?"

The radio was still running the same advisory: "wind . . . hail . . . tornado watch . . ."

He called to the horses, reached up from his chair and undid the latch, backing away as the gate swung open. Buster nuzzled his ear as he wheeled along beside them into the barn. Once inside he gave them each a scoop of oats. Usually he liked to linger here, thinking and talking, but as he felt the barn creak and moan under the wind, he turned himself back out to take another look.

He could hear now a continuous rumble of thunder and to the southwest the sky had turned a deep, deep blue. Here and there it was fractured by lightning. For a moment the wind stopped. The cackling of the hens, the snorting of the hogs, the chittering of the birds—all went silent. Then a sharp whistling rose up from somewhere. There was a worried nicker from Henry.

Jonathan looked again at the sky. And there he saw it, saw the strange, black thumb press itself down out of the bulging mass of clouds and stretch into a narrow tongue just licking over the surface of the ground.

Tornado!

It was so incredible that for a moment he simply stared. From the rise of the farmyard he watched the snakelike funnel slowly twist across the distant fields and broaden into a larger blackness. Before his eyes it became a black wall headed straight for the farm. Fear replaced amazement. He hurried back across the lot. The wind was shrieking now. But before he could get to the house, he heard horses.

 Looking back, there were Buster and Henry tearing madly around the inner lot. How could they have gotten out? He didn't know. And not just Buster, but Henry, pride and joy of his father's. Jonathan couldn't think if he had time or not, if it was safe or not.

He raced toward them, his arms aching with the effort. His hands burned against the friction of the rubber wheels. He didn't think he could push any harder, but the horses had to be saved. He had to save them for Dad.

First he had to get Buster calmed. If he could get him calmed, Henry would follow. He held out his sugar cubes. After circling and snorting around him, Buster came, and with Jonathan's hand on his neck, allowed himself to be calmed enough so that Jonathan could snap on a lead rope. He then did the same with Henry. On their leads they followed him back.

Inside, one stall was shattered from where Henry must have panicked and kicked. It must have been easy for Buster to force his latch and so race to join Henry.

To keep them safe from panic now Jonathan would have to stay, too, inside the barn and not below ground in the safety of the cellar. He'd glanced back as he got inside and the wall of the tornado seemed to be standing just outside the lot. It was a thing of sound now as much as of color, so loud that even though the horses' mouths were working, he could not hear them. Their frantic fidgeting took all his strength as he tried to control them by touch, by voice, by will.

He finally coaxed them into an old stall. It wouldn't be any stronger than the shattered one, but he knew nothing would be strong enough now, except him, his soothing them, his hands on them, the scent of sugar on his palms. This would be all that would keep them from bolting again.

The barn shook. Like a freight train the twister kept coming. The screaming wail of it was inside as well as outside, was inside him. And though he was drenched in sweat, he was freezing with goose bumps, too. Each second he expected to be his last.

Shading his eyes from the swirling chaff, he tried to squint through the slats of the siding to see. But it was darker than night, the electric gone now. There was just himself and the animals and the pounding of the storm, so deep, so strong, it felt as if the earth itself was shaking. The dried chaff and straw choked him and he gave up trying to keep his eyes open.

Cra-aaack! Whuumph! Suddenly hay swooshed down all over them. Keeping hold of both leads in one hand, Jonathan tried to move his chair out from under the beam that seemed to hang just over them. Finally he got to where he could see it resting on the cross bars above the stall. It could have killed them.

To work their way out he had to pull the hay loose from his wheelchair and then tug on the leads, tug and coax. It was then that he realized the thumping had stopped, the wind lessened and been joined by the pleasanter sound of rain. "We're saved," he shouted to Buster and Henry. "We're saved!"

All along the south side of the barn was a mess of hay and straw, small boards and other litter. The rain had settled to an easy shower and the sounds from the cattle sounded normal enough so he tied Buster and Henry to a post and wheeled himself outside.

What he saw took his breath away. The house had grown leaves, buried in the branches of the giant oak that had stood beside it. The barn's entire north side had collapsed. The haywagon, milking cans, feed buckets, Mom's bicycle, bird feeder, fences, clothesline had all changed places, gotten mixed up, twisted.

But it was when he looked beyond the house that his blood froze. Everything there was gone. Their hay barn, corncribs, hayrake, outbuildings, orchard, and—"ohh," Jonathan sucked in his breath, even the woods, the two-acre wood—it looked as if someone had gone through it with a scythe. He shook his head in disbelief. It was like something off the evening news. Incredibly the only thing left was a neatly stacked, four-foot pile of corn with hardly a splinter of wood to show that there had been a crib around it. A few chickens were already gathering around to claim their unlikely feast. He didn't notice that the rooster was not in his usual place at the head of his flock. The more he looked, the stranger it all seemed.

There was a feed bucket sitting on the slope of the house roof, perfectly, as if someone had set it there on purpose. Up in the elm that had remained standing, he could see one of the wheels from the haywagon, but no sign of the wagon itself. And sticking straight out from the front door of the house was a white slat from the picket fence driven straight in.

Finally, he turned back to the barn to check more carefully the other animals. Though he'd gone right past it, he hadn't seen the rooster lying on the ground like a dirty, crumpled rag. But when he picked it up and held the wet, limp body in his hands, he began to cry. He cried hard, and it wasn't like the crying we do when we're sad for someone we love. The rooster wasn't a pet. If anything, he was a bad-tempered, noisy, dumb bird. What mattered was that it was dead.

Jonathan knew then, at that moment, just how small he had been underneath the terrific power of the storm.

He lay the rooster down finally and started to see what he could do to really make sure the other animals were okay. Now that he had time to think more slowly, he also began to worry. Who could tell what else this storm had done? Mom and Dad—were they all right?

He heard them before he saw them—the honking of the horn and the rattling of Dad's truck through the soybeans. It was absolutely crazy. But everything this day had been crazy.

"Thank heavens you're all right," his mom said, climbing out and running to him and hugging him.

His dad was dead quiet for a long moment as he looked slowly around, but then he said, "Have a little bit of a storm here, Son?" and put his hand on Jonathan's shoulder. As Jonathan told them his story, he could see it all again, the blackness, the roaring of the wind, the funnel cloud, the cries of the animals, how he had to bring the horses in and stay, the battering of the barn itself. They listened. They didn't scold or baby him. He felt better than he had for a long time. He knew he had done a thing he could feel good about.

He wouldn't care so much now when people looked at him. He knew they would. They would still see his "condition," but when they knew this story they might begin to see a lot more. They might just see him. Jonathan.

For Jared Carter who said it needed to be done.   MH

To my younger brother, Nick.   MM

Acknowledgment

Thanks to Nancy Springer and Anna Smucker.   MH

Text copyright © 1995 by Marc Harshman
Illustrations copyright © 1995 by Mark Mohr
All rights reserved. No part of this book may be reproduced
in any form without permission in writing from the Publisher.
Library of Congress Cataloging-in-Publication Data
Harshman, Marc.
The storm / Marc Harshman ; illustrated by Mark Mohr.
p.   cm.
Summary: Though confined to a wheelchair, Jonathan
faces the terror of a tornado all by himself and saves
the lives of the horses on the family farm.
ISBN 0-525-65150-0
[1. Physically handicapped—Fiction.   2. Tornadoes—Fiction.
3. Farm life—Fiction.]   I. Mohr, Mark, ill.   II. Title.
PZ7.H256247Sm   1995 [Fic]—dc20   94-4894   CIP   AC
Published in the United States of America by Cobblehill Books,
an affiliate of Dutton Children's Books, a division of
Penguin Books USA Inc., 375 Hudson Street, New York, New York 10014
Designed by Kathleen Westray
Printed in Hong Kong
First Edition 10 9 8 7 6 5 4 3 2 1

WASHOE COUNTY LIBRARY
RENO, NEVADA